The Big Purple Cat

Elizabeth Hamilton

AuthorHouse™ UK
1663 Liberty Drive
Bloomington, IN 47403 USA
www.authorhouse.co.uk
Phone: 0800.197.4150

© 2019 Elizabeth Hamilton. All rights reserved.

No part of this book may be reproduced, stored in a retrieval system, or transmitted by any means without the written permission of the author.

Published by AuthorHouse 01/28/2019

ISBN: 978-1-7283-8410-8 (sc)
ISBN: 978-1-7283-8411-5 (e)

Print information available on the last page.

Any people depicted in stock imagery provided by Getty Images are models,
and such images are being used for illustrative purposes only.
Certain stock imagery © Getty Images.

This book is printed on acid-free paper.

Because of the dynamic nature of the internet, any web addresses or links contained in this book may have changed since publication and may no longer be valid. The views expressed in this work are solely those of the author and do not necessarily reflect the views of the publisher, and the publisher hereby disclaims any responsibility for them.

authorHOUSE®

The Big Purple Cat

Once upon a time far away in the country side lived a big purple cat. He had a diamond collar around his neck and a big red bow also. He was a very proud cat.

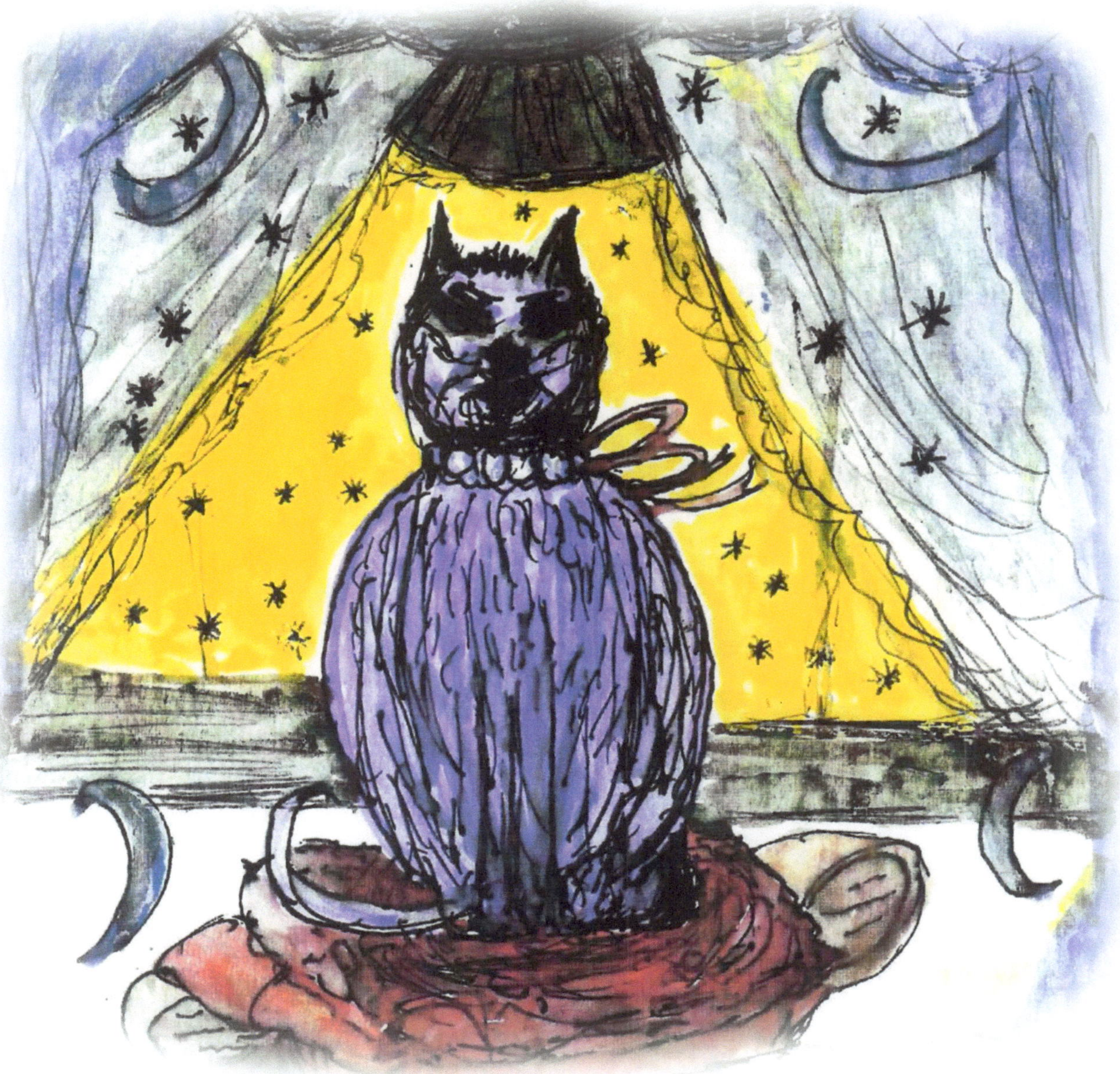

He lived in a big old house in the country with a little old lady. She was very strange. She did her own thing, 'because like'.

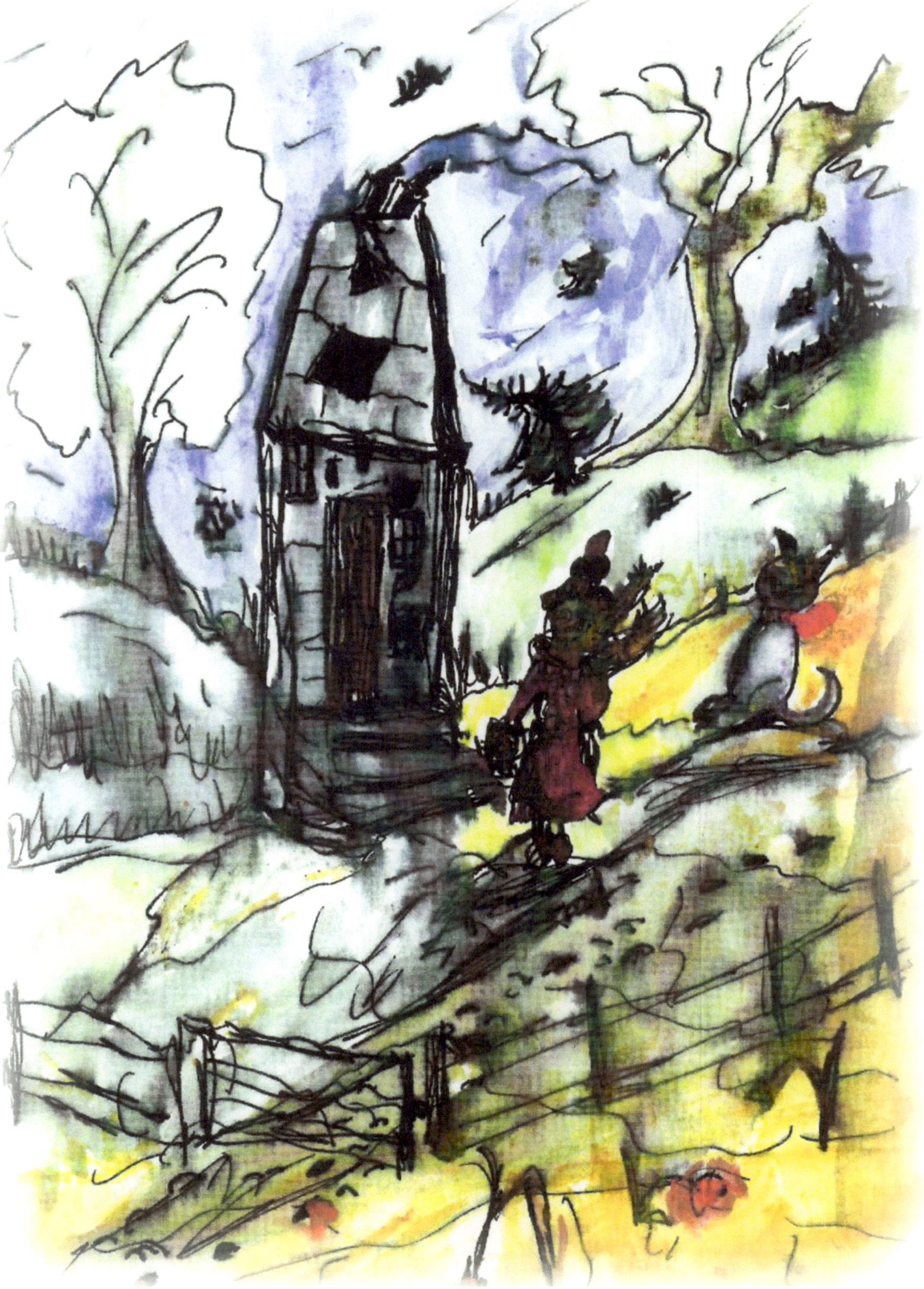

One day the old lady went to France (just like that!) to visit her sister. She sailed away on a big boat and left BigPurpleCat on his own.

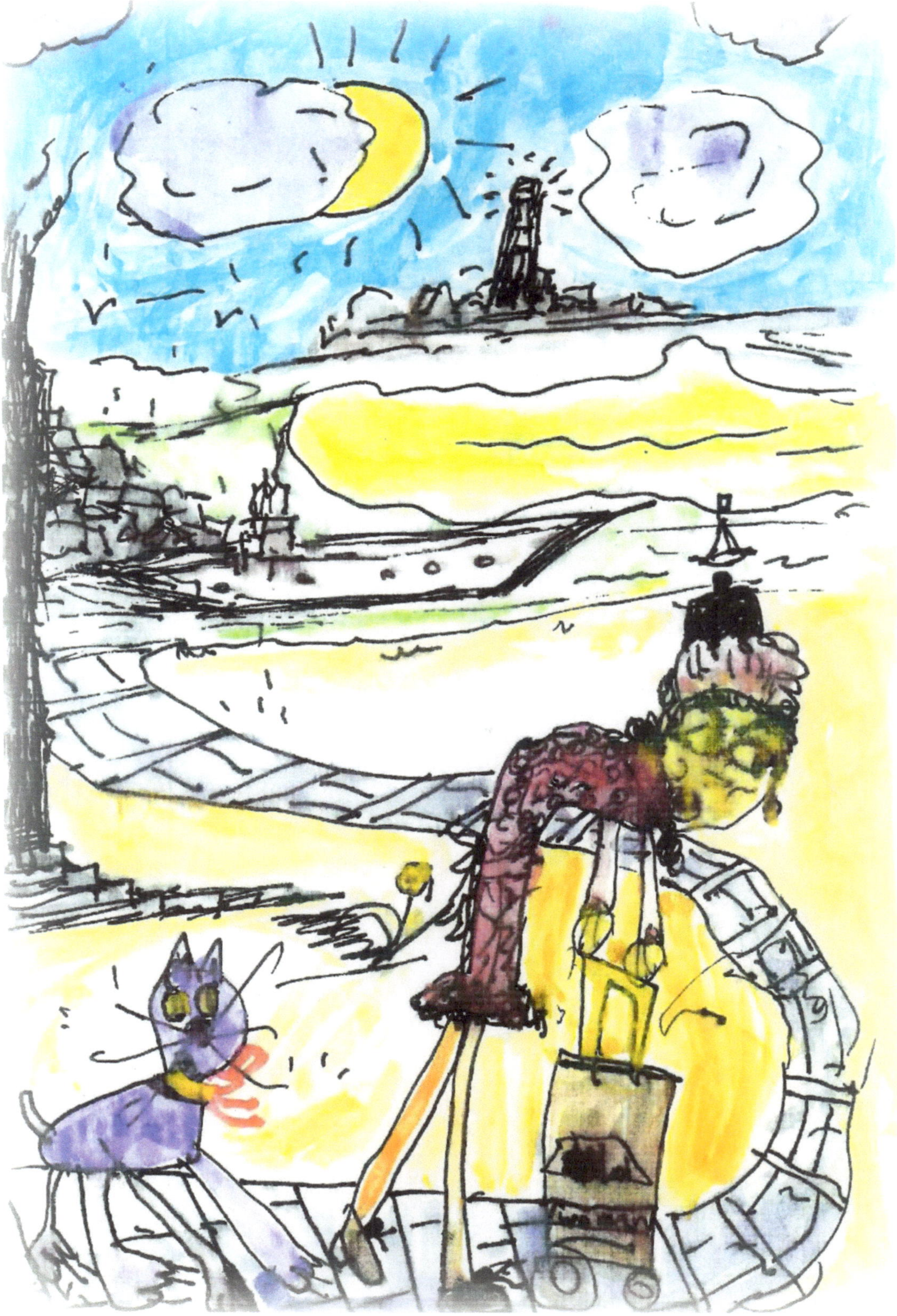

He was very hungry as there was no food left in the house. The slates fell off the roof and the snow and the rain came in and fell on BigPurpleCat's lovely fur. The big purple cat decided to leave the house. Could anyone blame him? No, i don't think so!

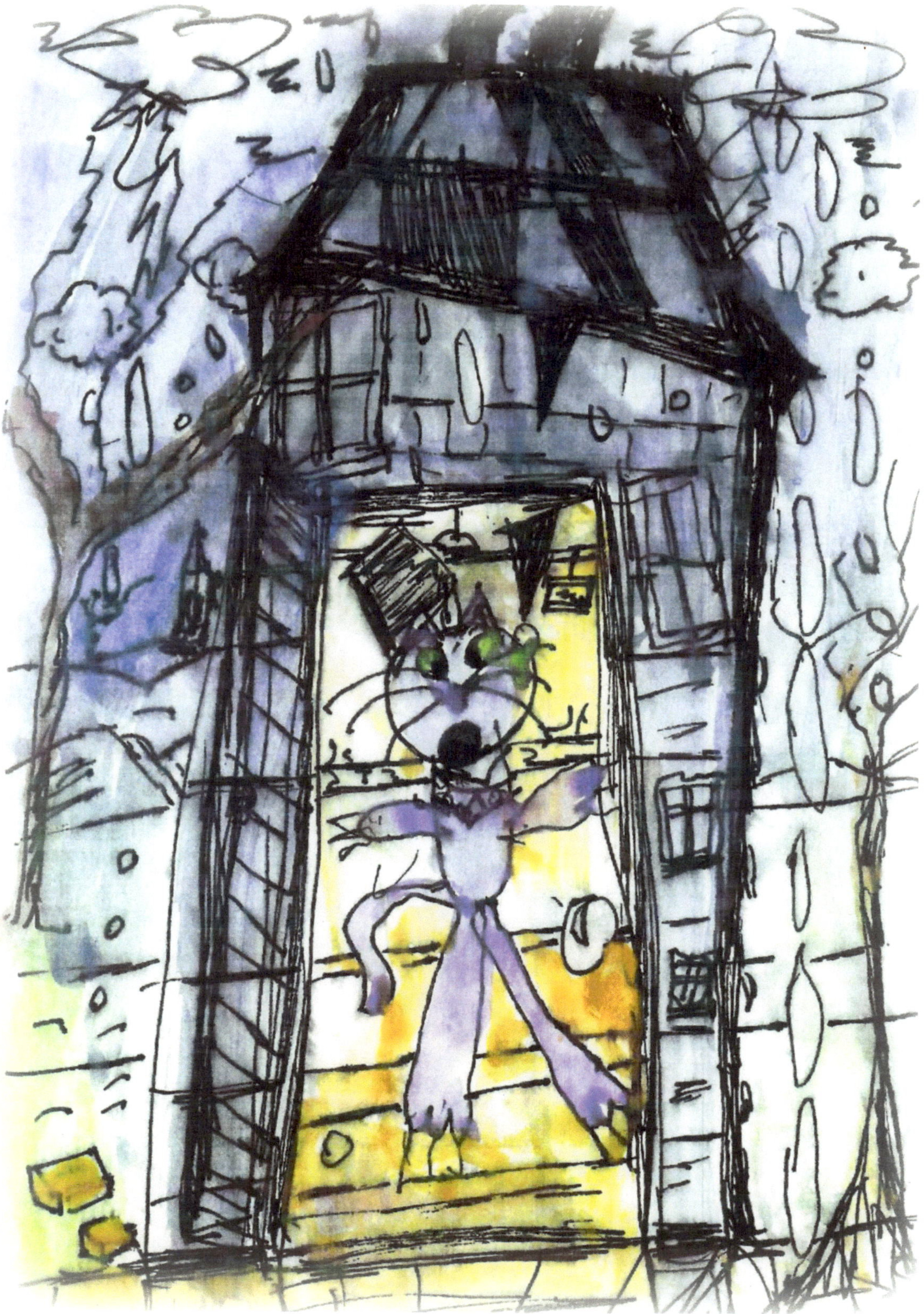

He walked for miles and miles along the country roads, through the fields and rain and howling winds and snow. The big winter lion in the sky blew a big storm all around. The leaves were blowing all around and pieces of twigs were being hurled at poor cat.

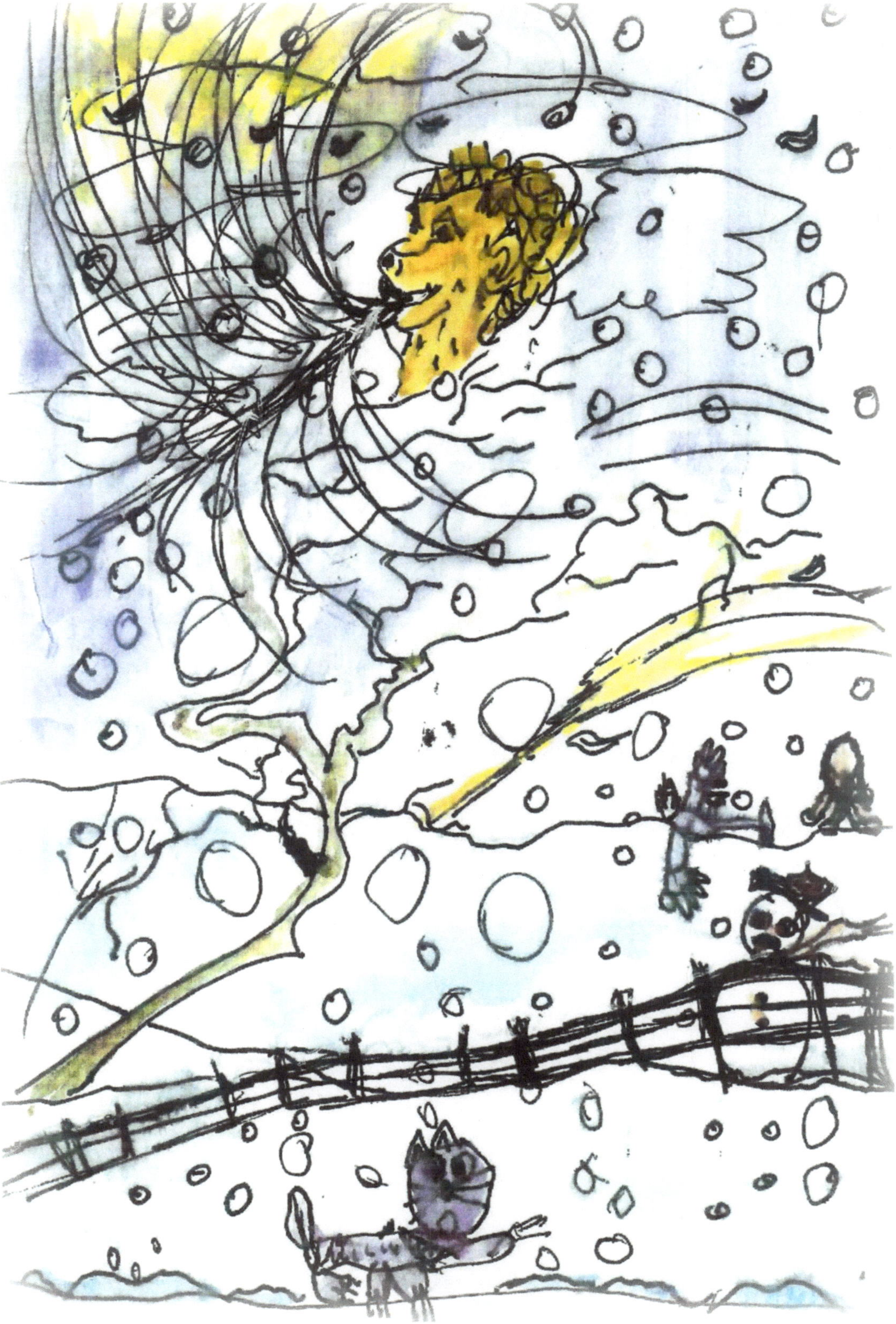

His beautiful green eyes were sore from squinting against the wind. He walked until he came to a crossroads and had to stop for a rest. He saw an old farmhouse with a big bare leafed tree beside it. He climbed up into the tree and stayed there, shivering all afternoon. It was starting to get dark.

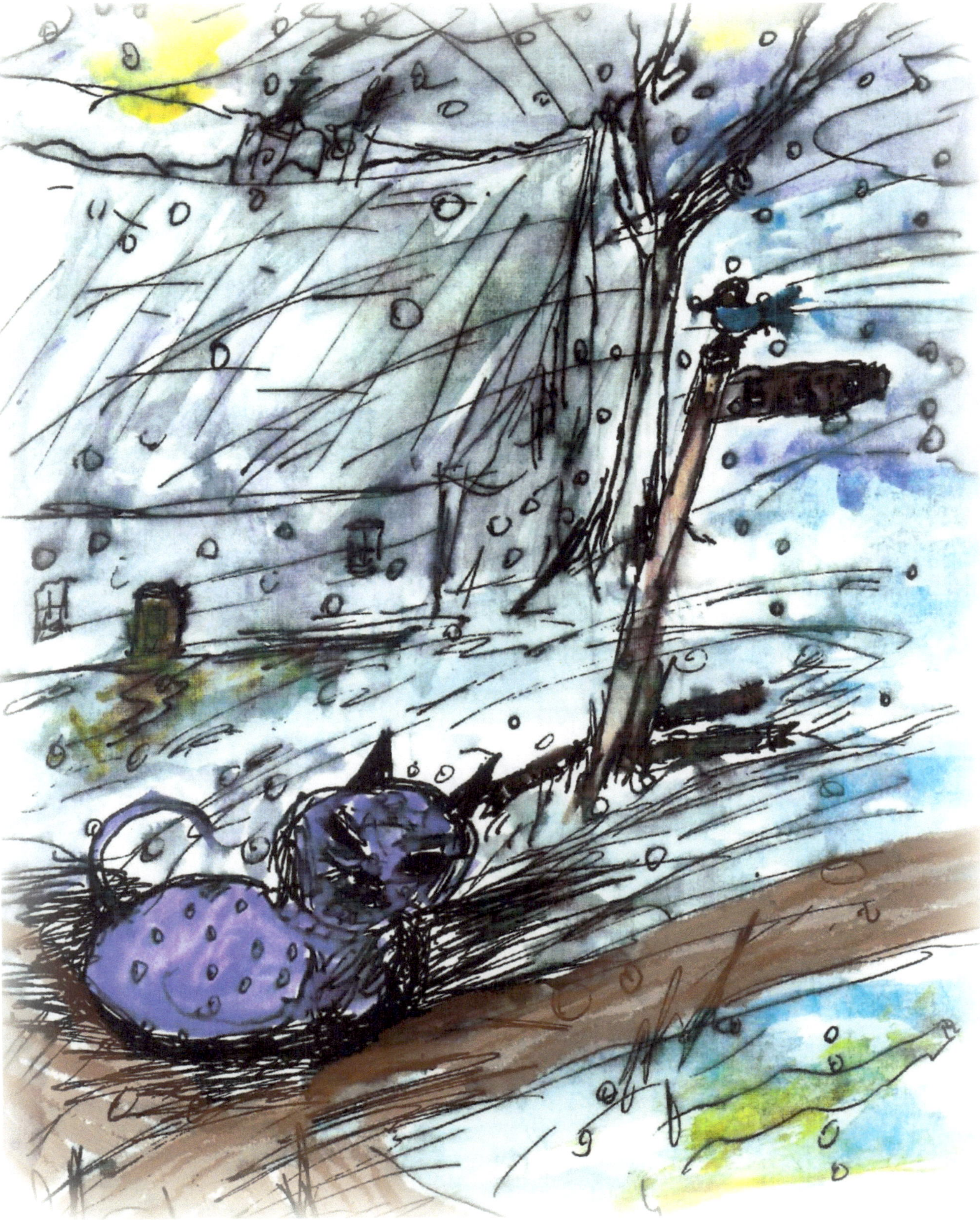

The clouds were hurrying by. Even they wanted to get home. Miranda and George walked through the farmyard carrying logs for the fire. Suddenly they heard a loud sound, "Meaooooowww".

"What's that sound?", they said, looking at one another with surprise. They looked up and saw PurpleCat in the tree.

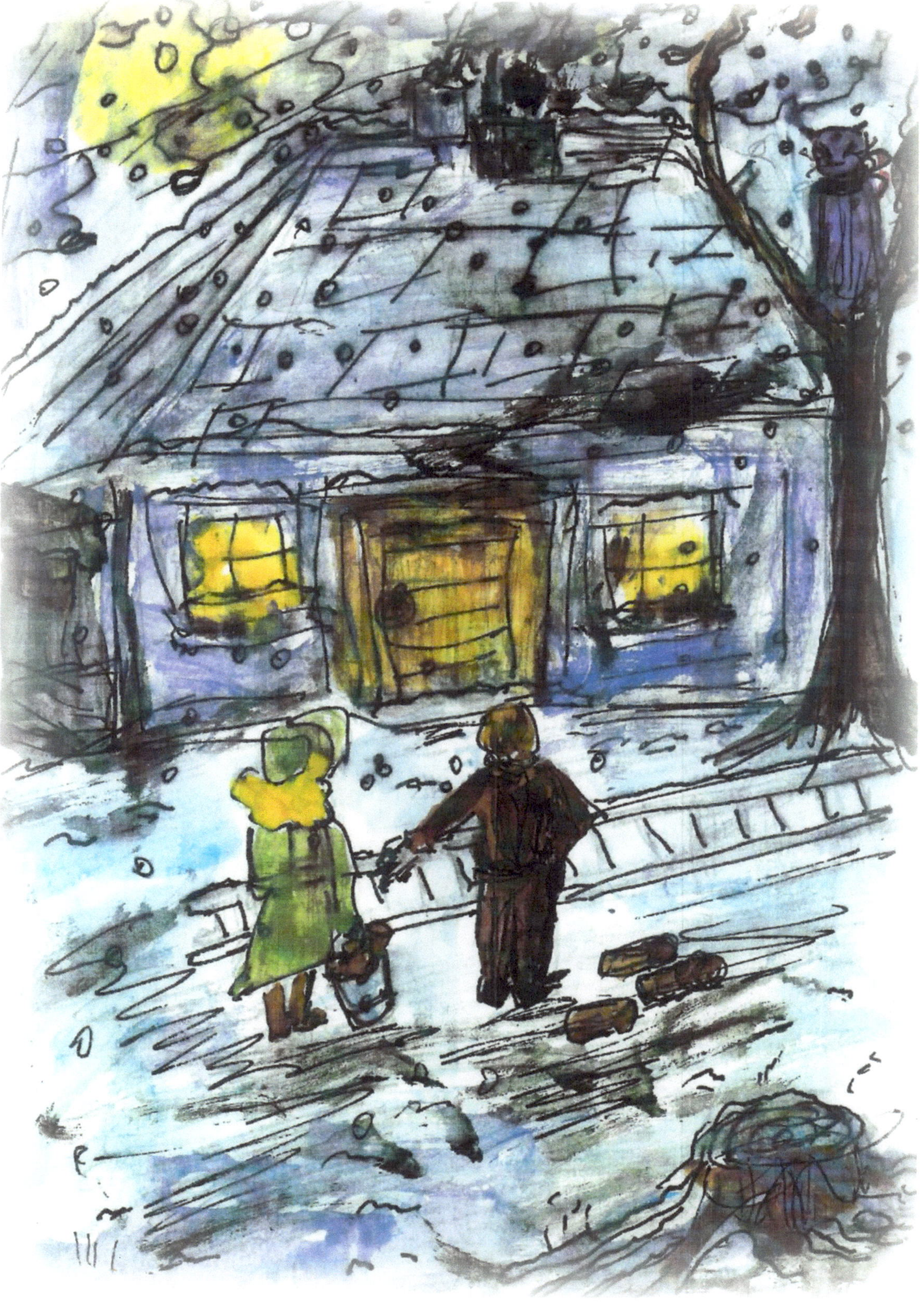

They got a ladder from the barn and got him down. They went into the farmhouse where their Dad was sitting at the fire.

"We found a big purple cat in the tree. He is tired and hungry. Can we keep him please?" Dad looked at Miranda and George, and then he looked at the BigPurpleCat. Finally he said "if he behaves himself, you can!"

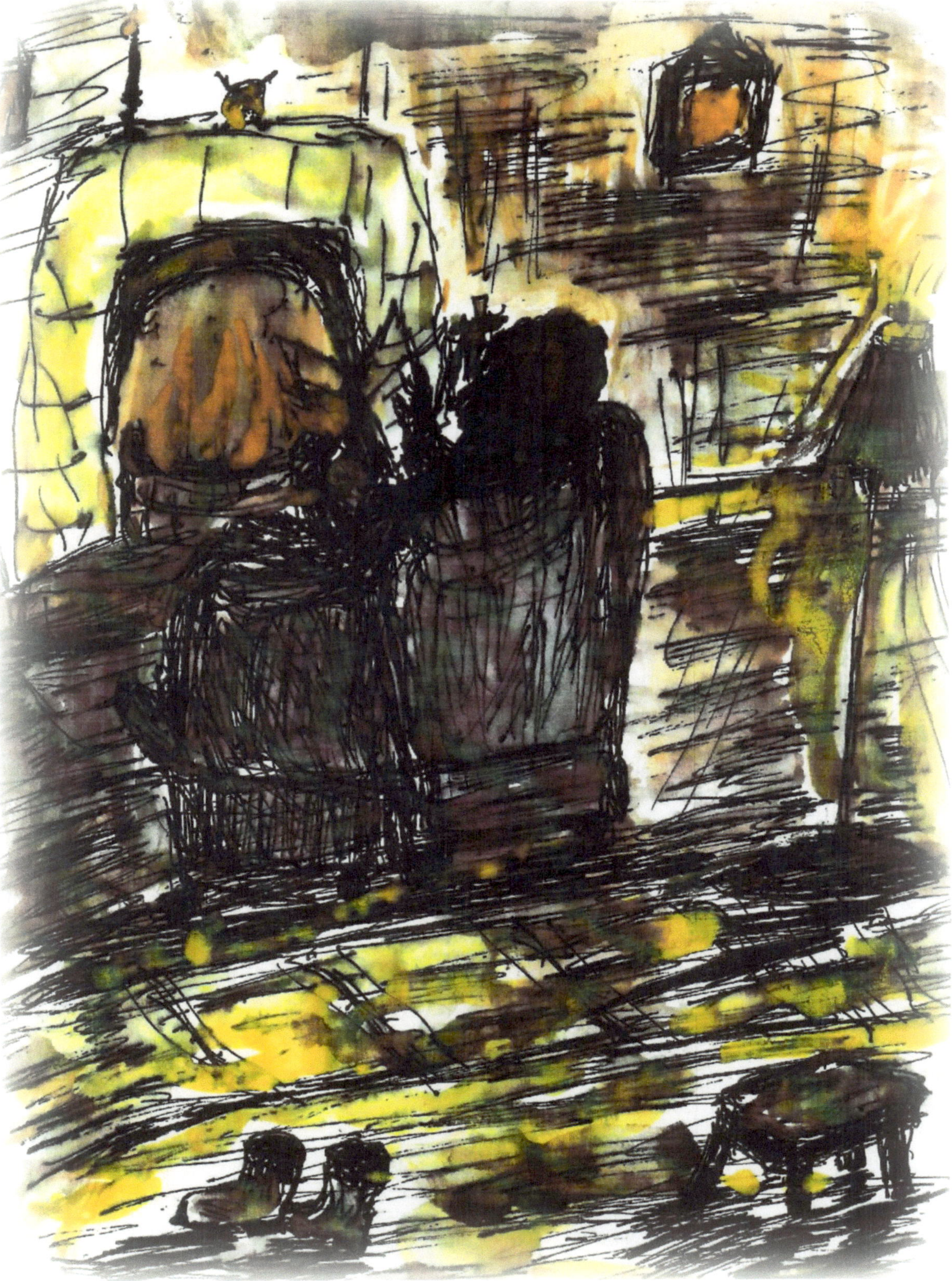

"Bring him into the kitchen". Dad said turning back to his newspaper. Miranda and George were delighted. They put him in front of the fire in a big basket with a big red cushion inside. Then they dried him with a big fluffy pink towel. He was now warm and dry. They gave him six sausages and a big bowl of fresh cream. BigPurpleCat had a lovely sleep that night and was so happy.

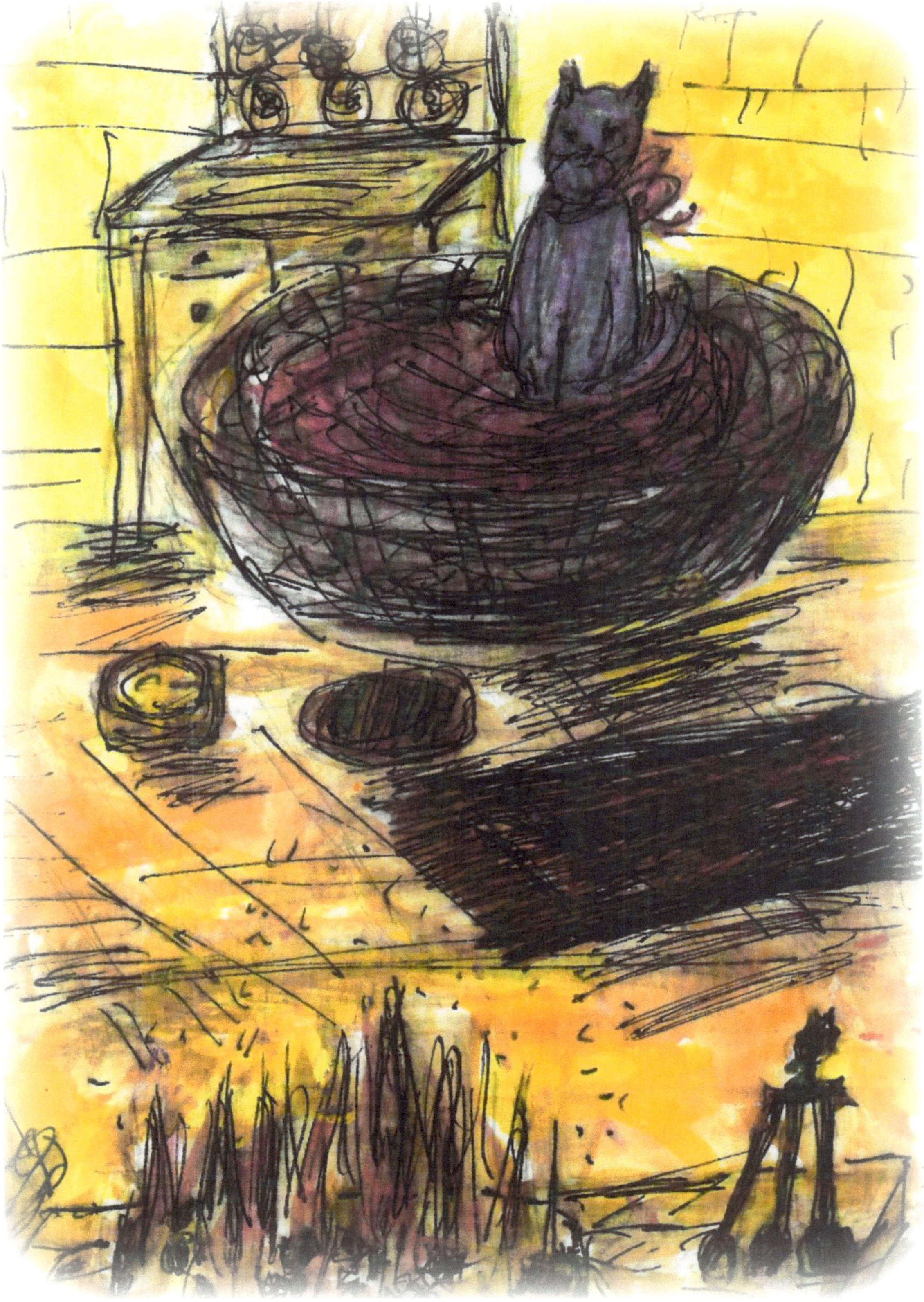

For the next few weeks he was glad to stay at the farmhouse being pampered, but as the days passed he grew restless.

One day he thought, "I'm fed up with all of this 'namby pamby' stuff. I'm going to do my own thing. After all, I am BigPurpleCat. And I don't have to answer to anyone, especially humans".

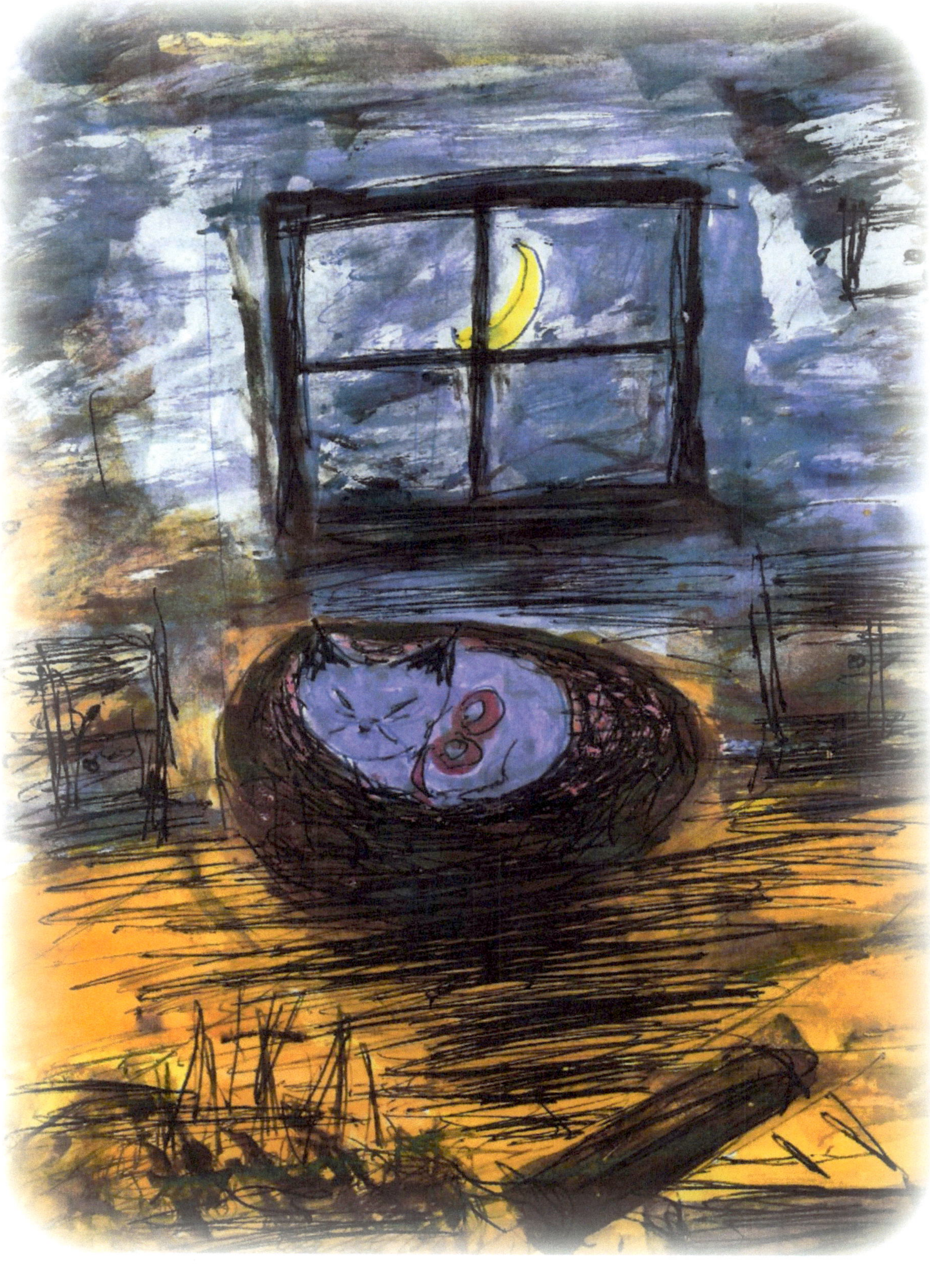

When everyone had gone to sleep that night, he crept into Miranda's room and took her overnight case and sunglasses. The next morning as the sun rose, PurpleCat crept out through the hedge carrying the overnight case in his mouth and wearing Miranda's sunglasses as a disguise.

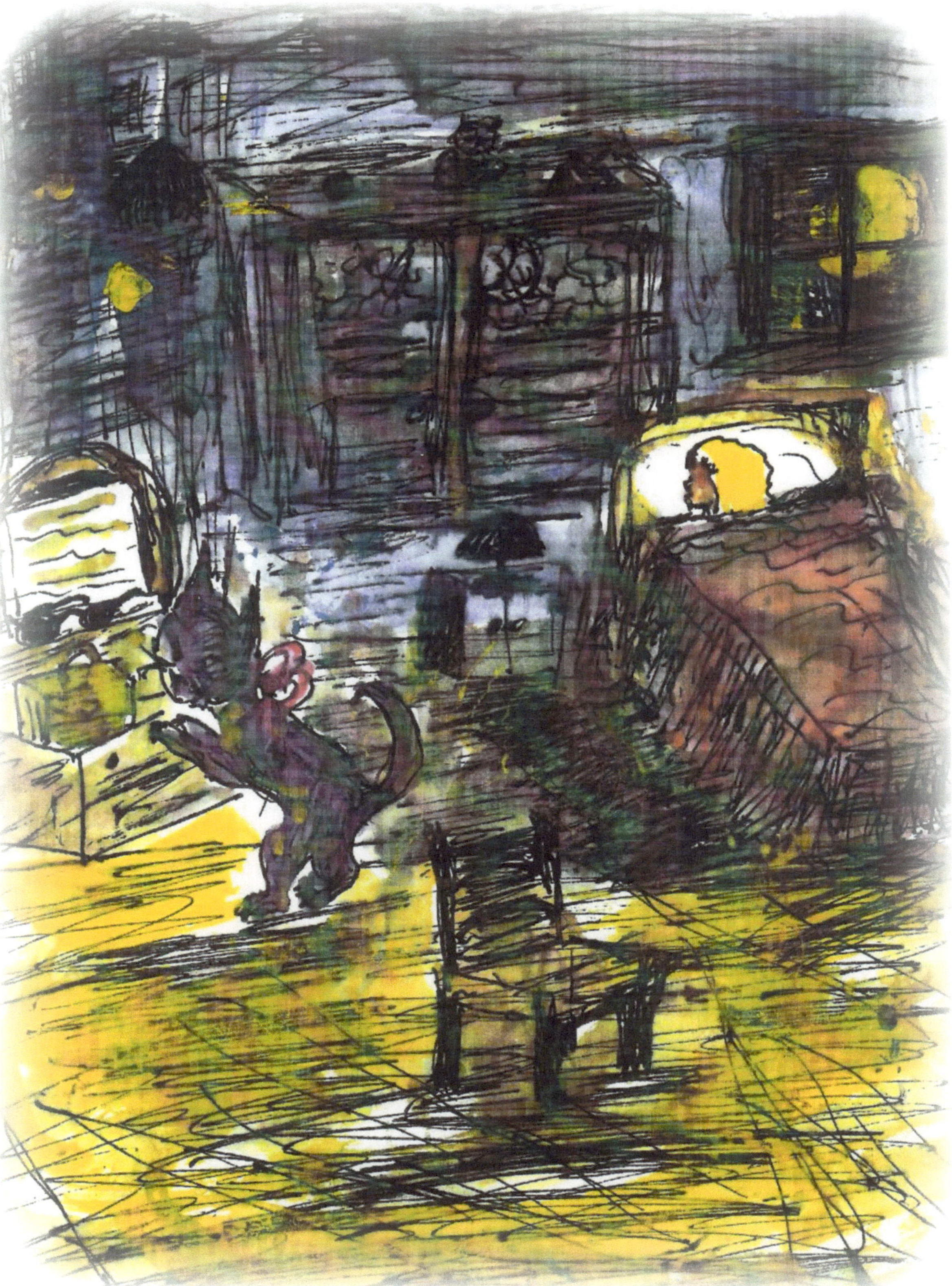

The only ones to notice him leaving were the ducks and hens in the yard who were shocked to see him sneaking away. "He is a very selfish cat", said one of the ducks to the hens. "All cats are selfish", replied one of the hens snootily. "Not all of them", said the duck, "just some".

"The sun is shining, it's a lovely day and I am going in a big adventure and I might not come back at all. Only if it suits me". Thought PurpleCat ignoring them.

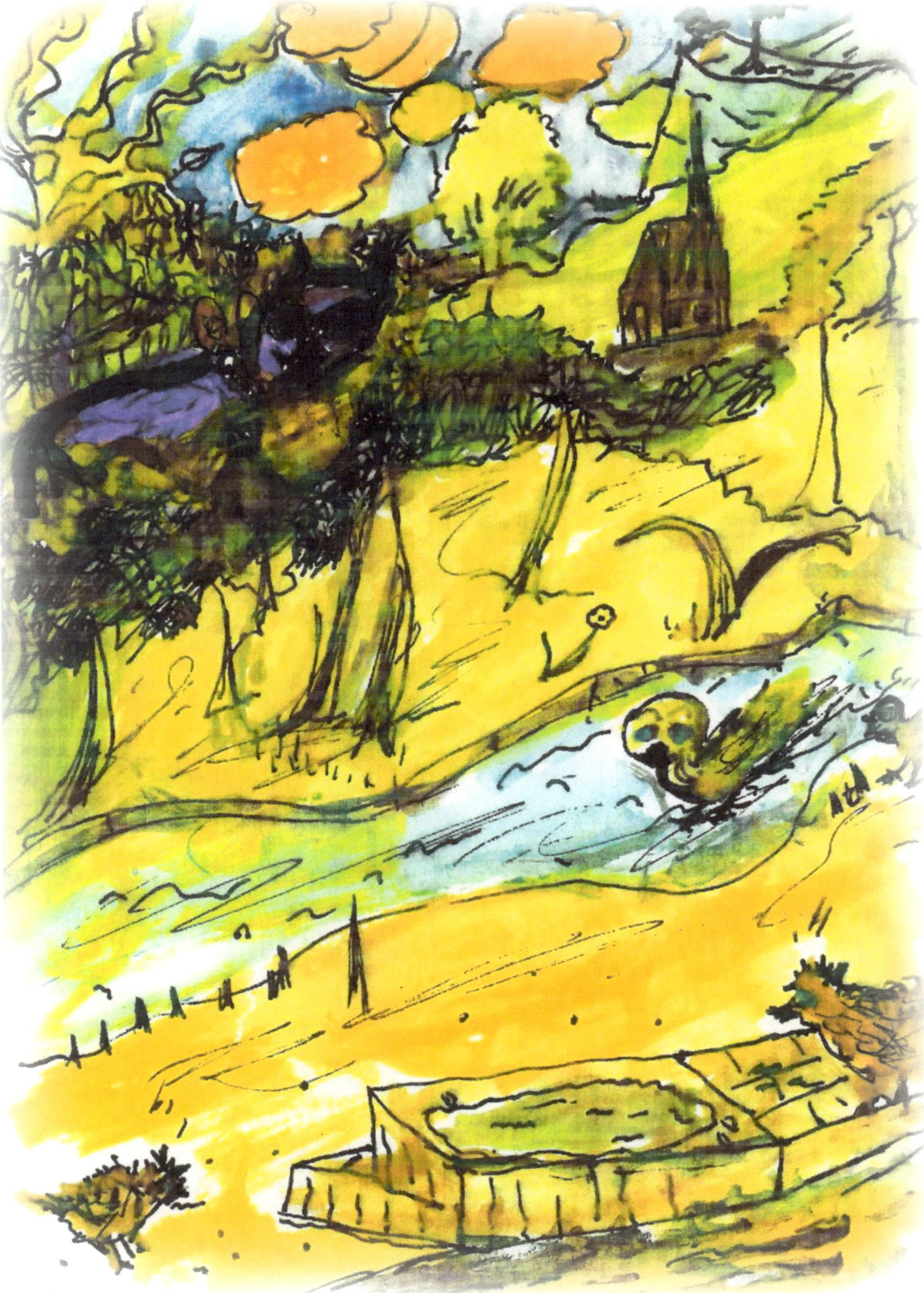

He did not know it was still only a winter sun shining and glinting through the trees. It was still a long time before spring would return. He whistled and sang as he went through a lovely green field at the side of a wood. "This is great". He said to the birds as he sat down to have a snack. He enjoyed sausages and a bottle of fresh cream he had taken from the kitchen while everyone was sleeping. He was so busy eating and enjoying himself that he did not notice the dark heavy clouds gathering overhead.

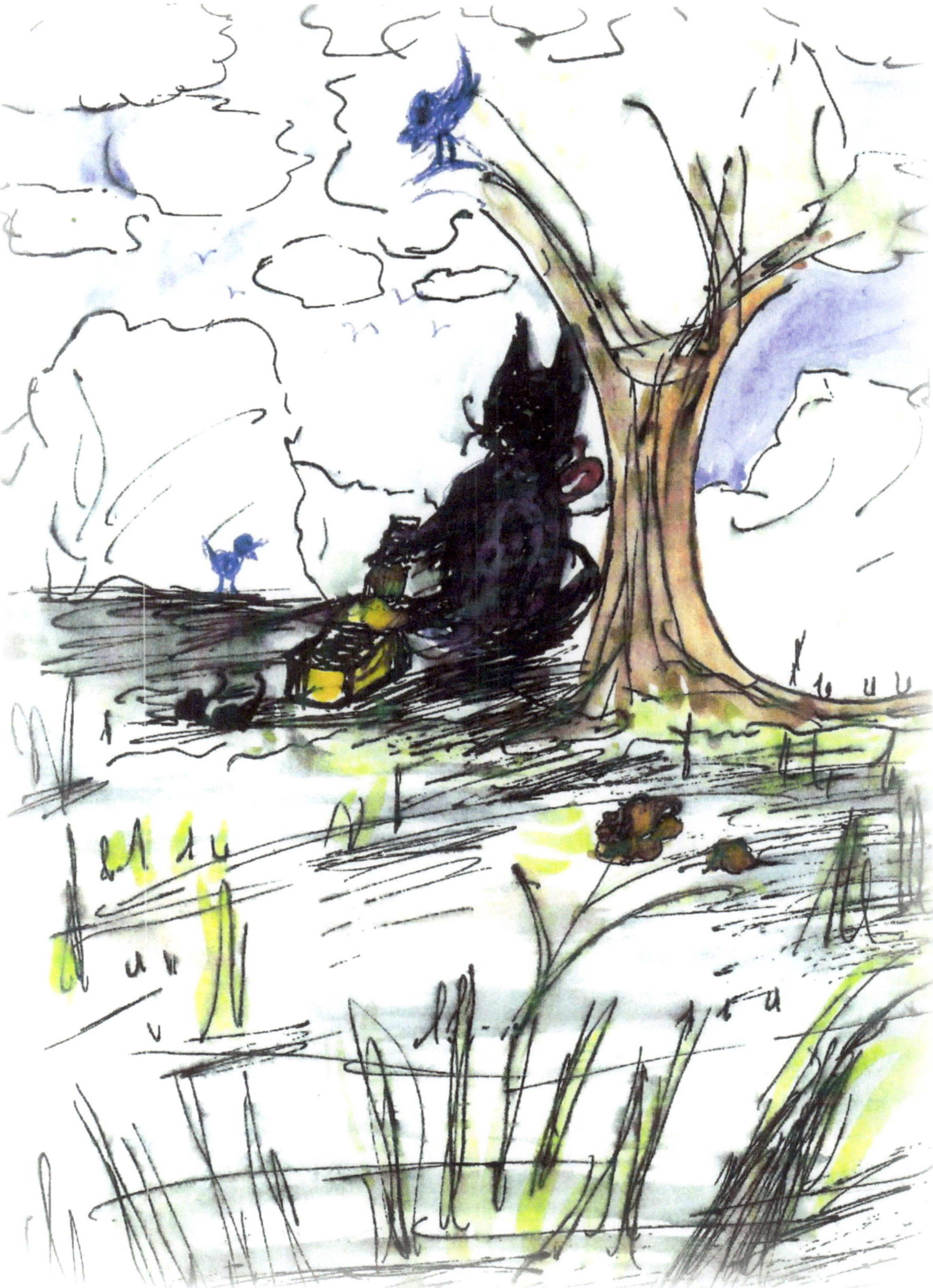

it began to rain and the wind started to blow and when he went into the woods for shelter the rain and the wind still found him through the trees. PurpleCat fell into a very, very large puddle. it was almost a small pool. imagine! He dropped the overnight case as well as the sunglasses and they sank to the bottom of the puddle without a sound.

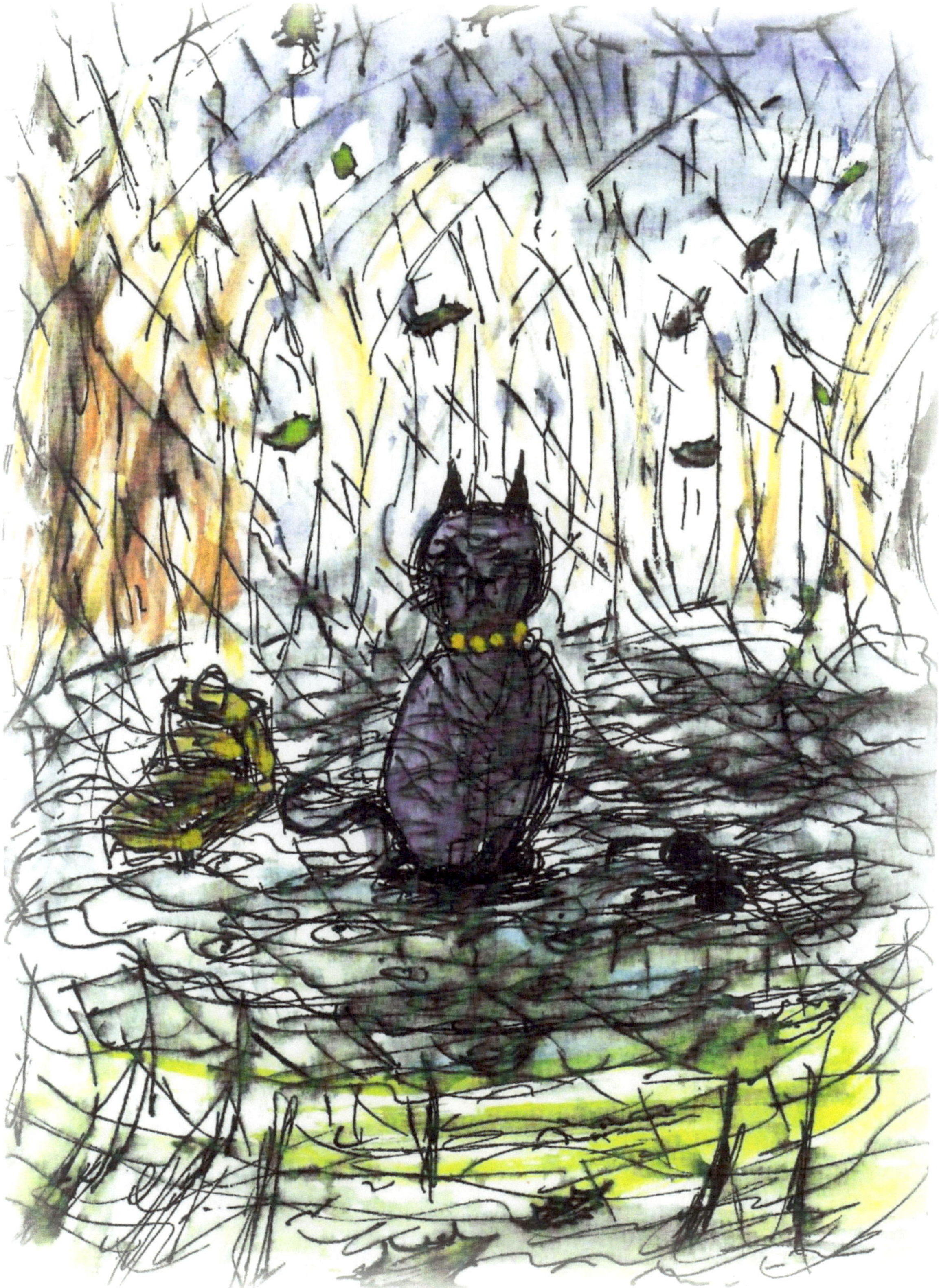

The only dry place he could find was a hollow at the bottom of a very old tree. "I wish I had not left Miranda and George", he thought as he tried to stay dry in the middle of the cold dark night. It was very scary. PurpleCat was feeling very frightened, being on his own in the dark with all the strange noises in the wood and the branches of the old tree creaking above his head. "If I got back to the farmhouse safely, I would never leave my family again", he said. He gave a big sigh as raindrops fell off of the big branches above and landed on this snooty nose.

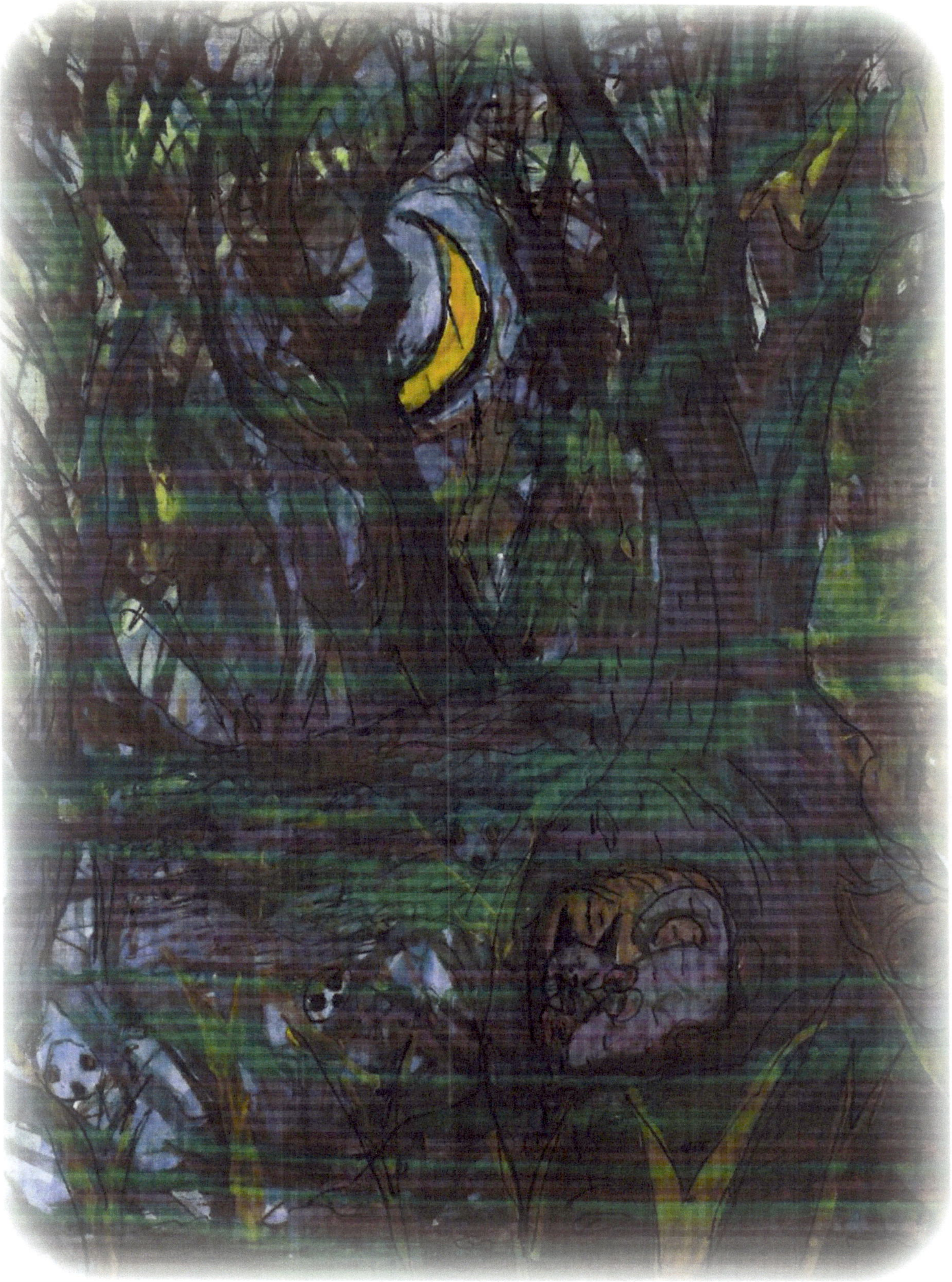

In the meantime, Miranda and George were searching everywhere for BigPurpleCat in the rain. "PurpleCat, PurpleCat!" they called out. There was no answer and as the darkness came they had to go home without the BigPurpleCat. They were very sad. The next morning they set off very early again to look for PurpleCat.

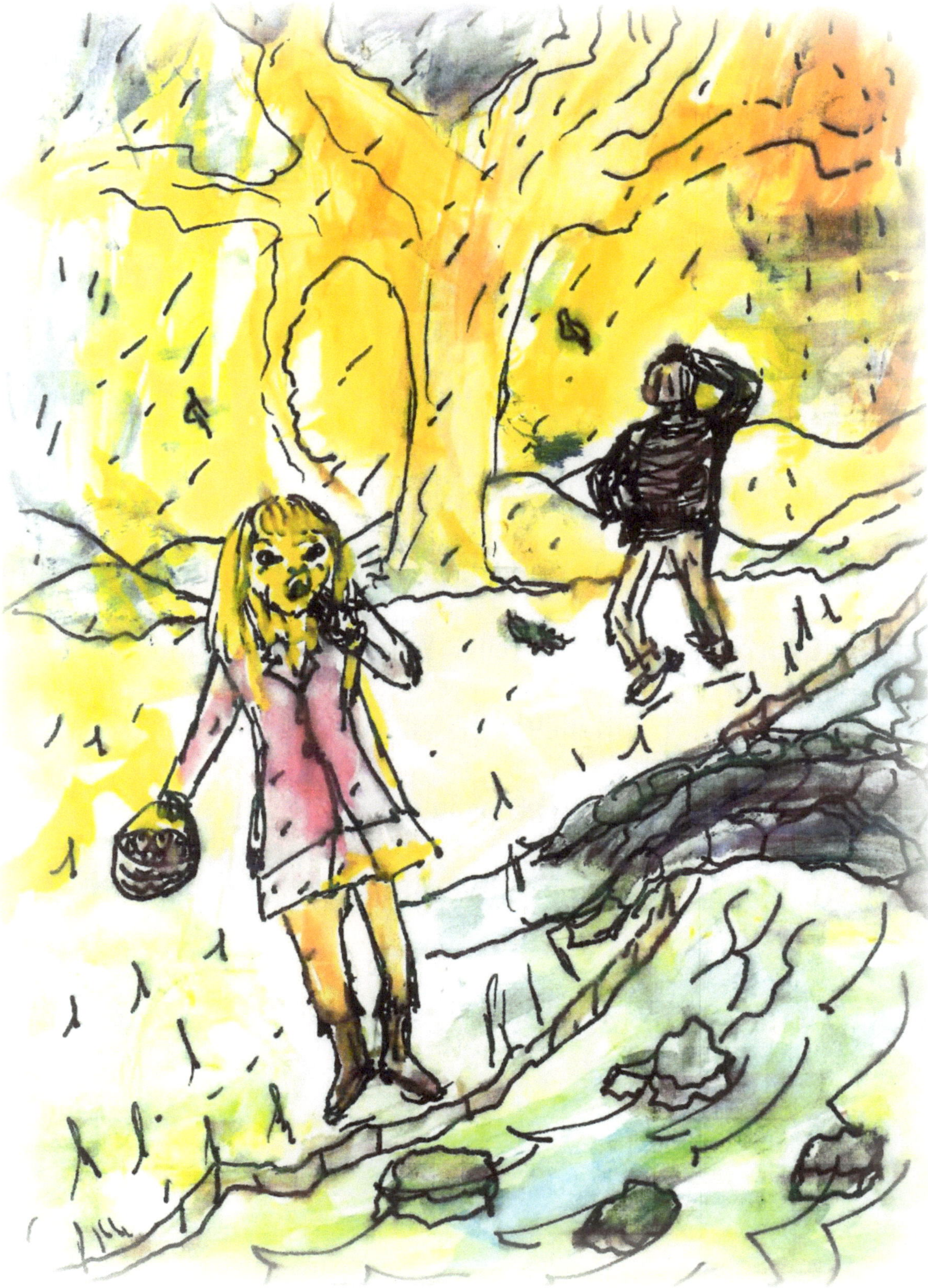

After walking a very long way and calling for PurpleCat the whole time, they heard a very faint "Meeooooow". They found BigPurpleCat sitting on a tree stump crying. Miranda knelt down and wiped his tears with a tissue. "I am so sorry", said PurpleCat. "I will never leave you again". "It's ok", said George, patting him on the head. "We are all selfish at times, but we still love you". "I love you too", said BigPurpleCat

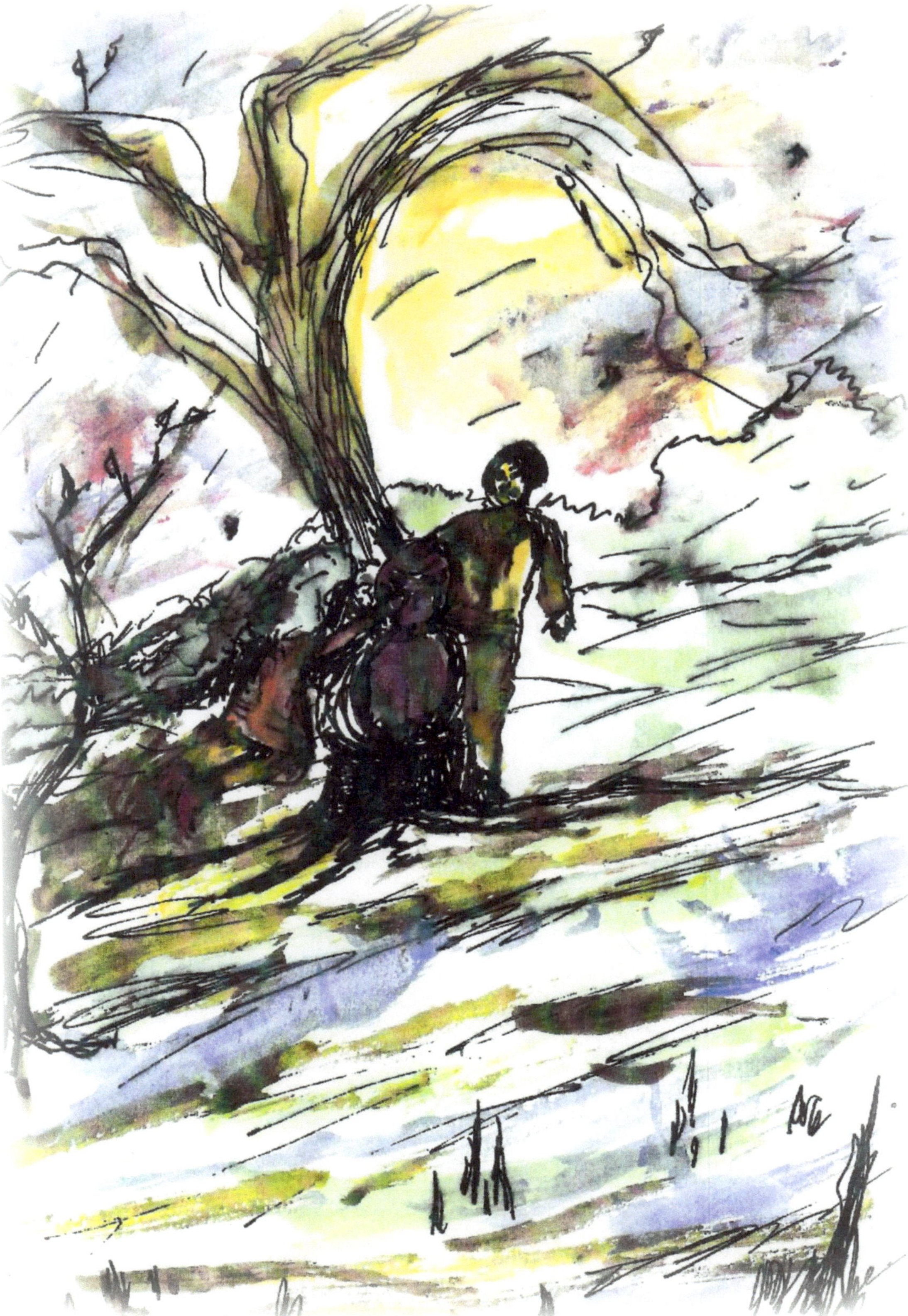

They all trudged home. They were very tired but very happy to be back together again and heading back to the cozy farmhouse especially now that it had started to snow again.

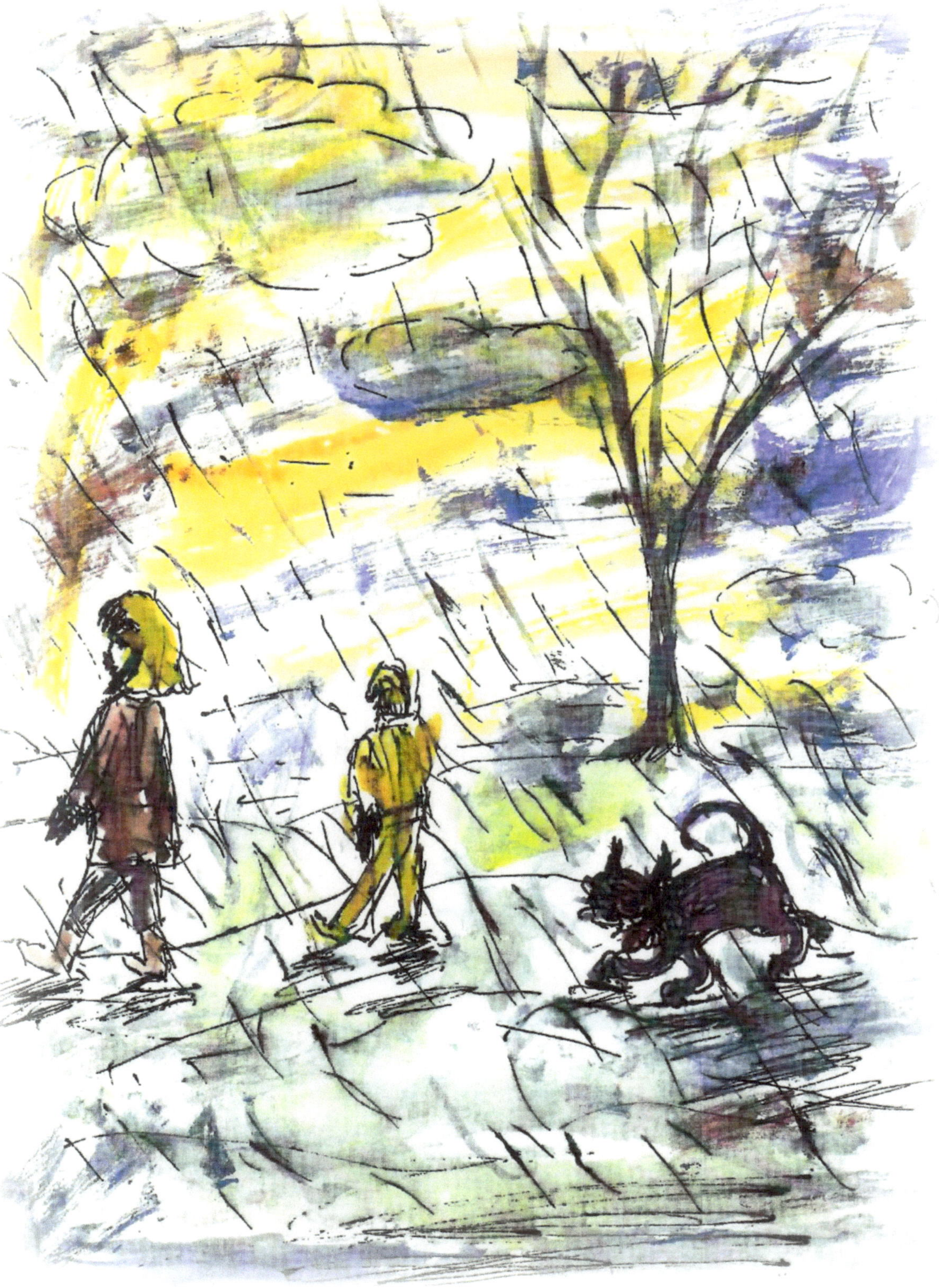

Everyone was so delighted to have BigPurpleCat back home that they all had a big party for him. Miranda and George's Mom made a big cake with a candle on it. It was a great party.

PurpleCat jumped up on the mantelpiece and knocked down the clock and the candlesticks but he did not care.

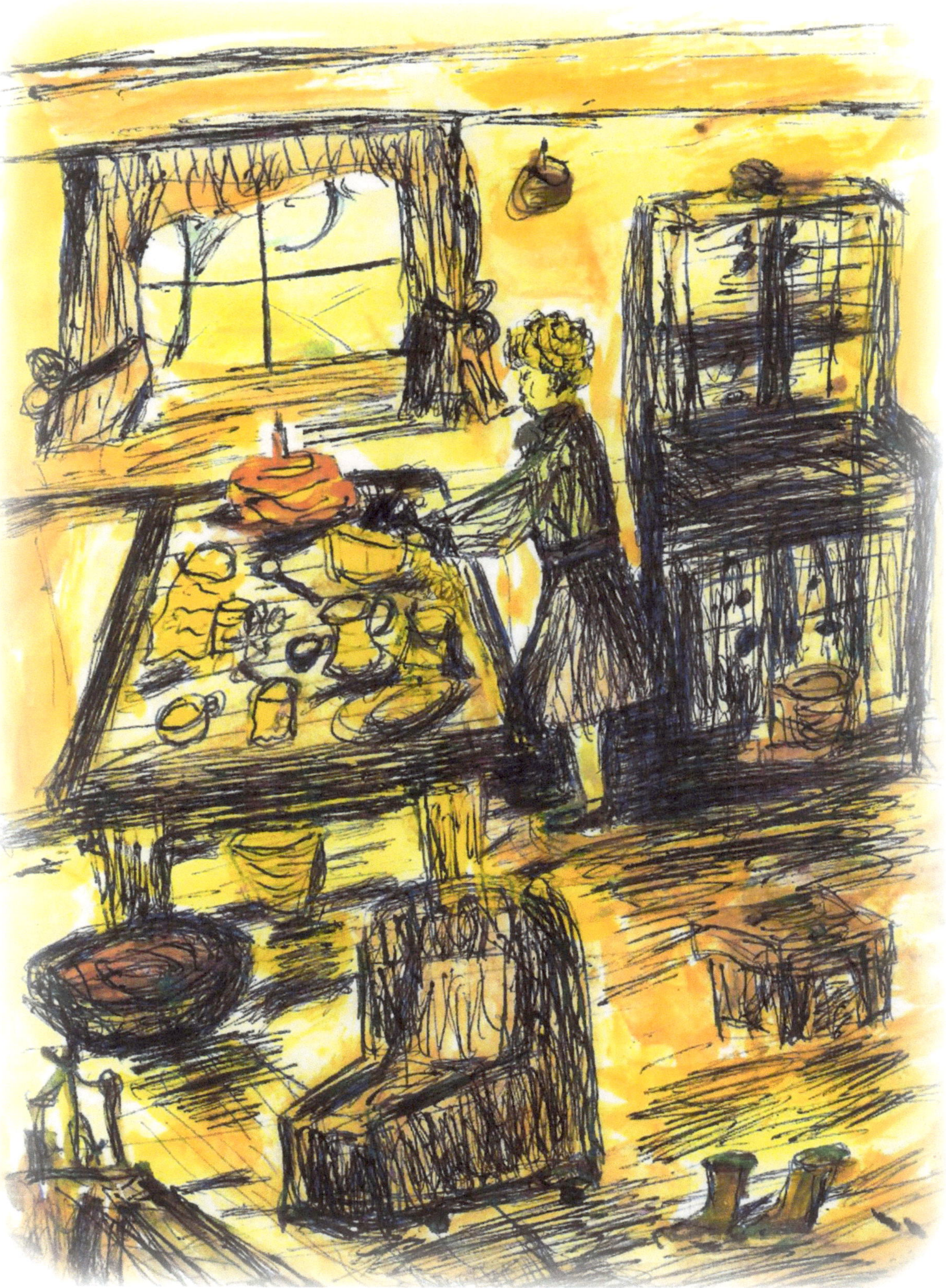

He wanted everyone to see him. He wanted to be the "*king of the castle*".

"I'll be good from now on!" he purred loudly, but there was a glint in his green eyes as he said this.

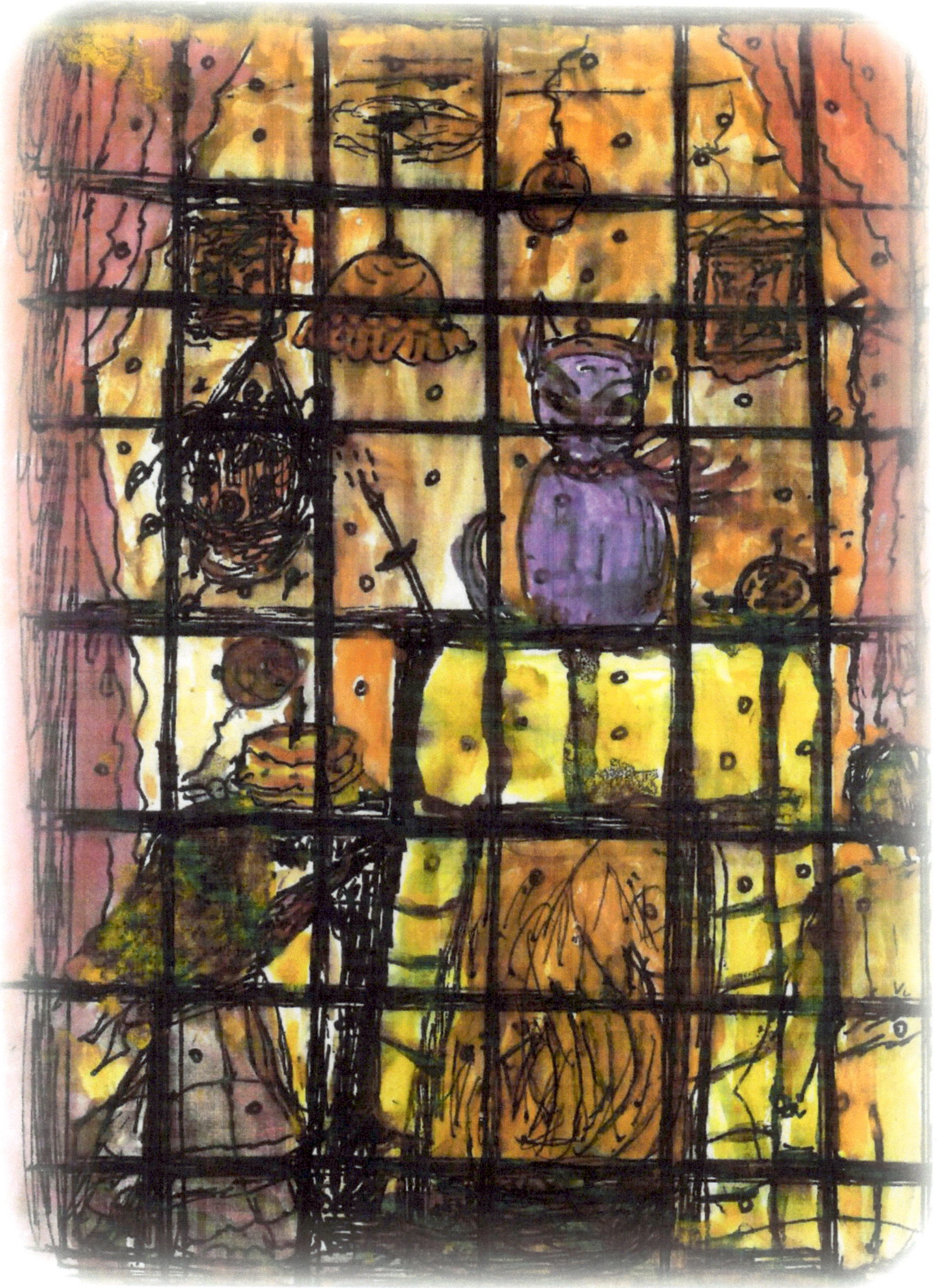

Even though he wanted to be good, i think, BigPurpleCat was already planning his next adventure!

Alas, he is a very secretive cat and we will just have to wait and see.

The End.

THE END

CPSIA information can be obtained
at www.ICGtesting.com
Printed in the USA
BVHW020813150319
542768BV00003B/21/P

9 781728 384108